# MY CAT,
# THE SILLIEST CAT
# IN THE WORLD

# MY

Abrams Books for Young Readers
New York

# CAT

## THE SILLIEST CAT IN THE WORLD

written and illustrated by **GILLES BACHELET**

Designer: Angela Carlino
Production Manager: Colin Hough-Trapp

Library of Congress Cataloging-in-Publication data has been applied for.
ISBN 0-8109-4913-X

Printed and bound in Belgium by Proost
10 9 8 7 6 5 4 3 2

**HNA**
**harry n. abrams, inc.**
a subsidiary of La Martinière Groupe
115 West 18th Street
New York, NY 10011
www.hnabooks.com

J
E
Bachelet

My cat is very fat, very sweet,
and very, very silly.

 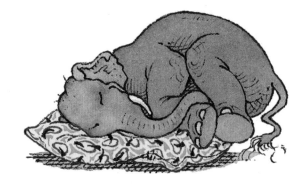 

When my cat's not eating, he's sleeping.

When he's not sleeping, he's eating.

When he's not eating, he's sleeping.

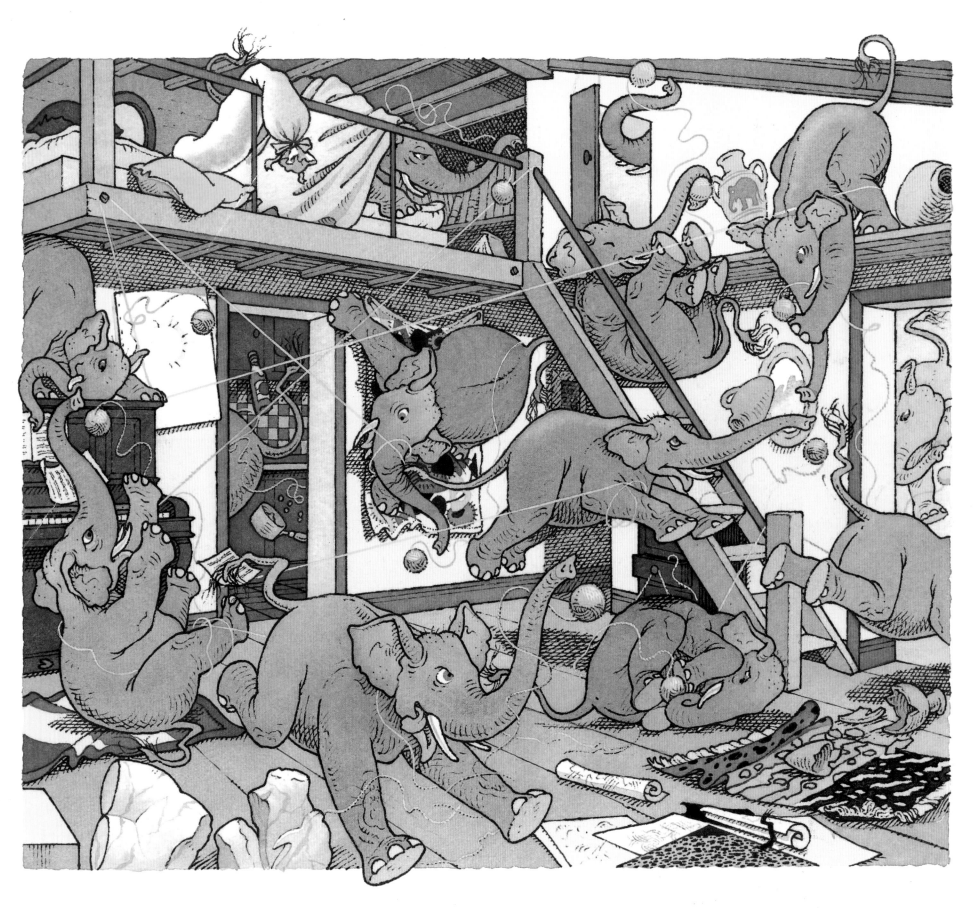

In rare instances, my cat devotes several minutes to exercise.

When my cat's asleep on the couch, I have to warn guests
that he's not just another cushion.

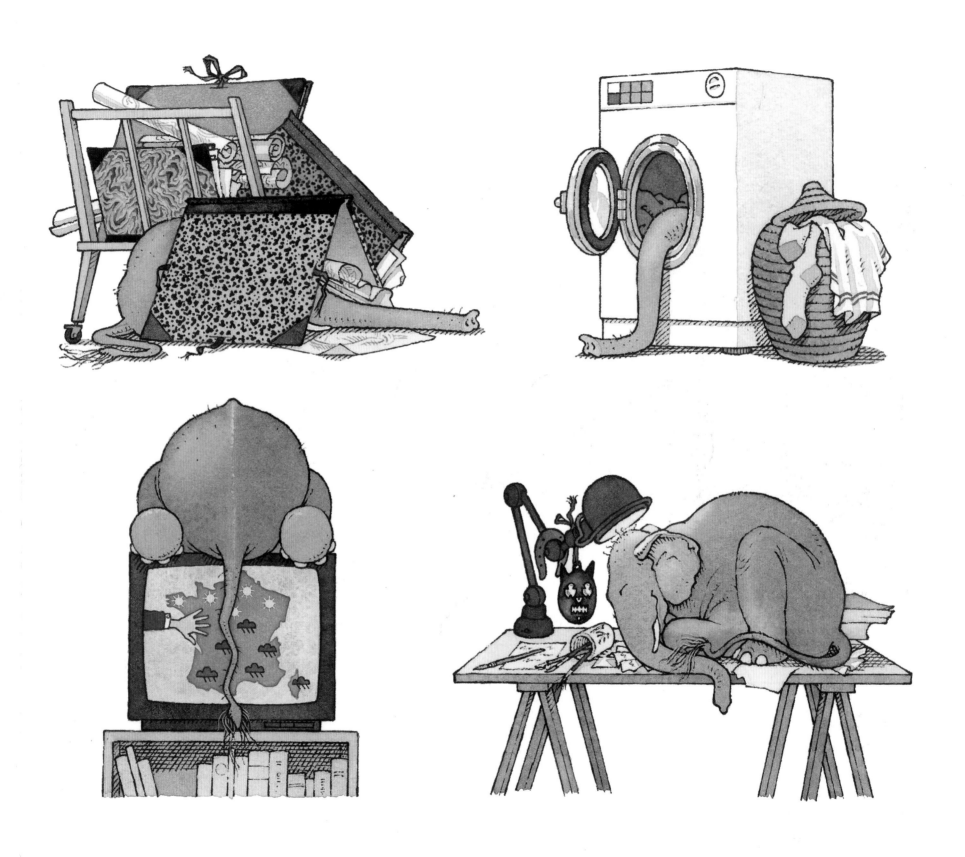

But for the most part, my cat can sleep just fine without the couch.

If I don't pour his food directly into his bowl, my cat
may actually starve to death right in front of an open box of treats.

Gilles Bachelet
Illustrator

Director
Museum of Natural History
U.S.A.

Dear Sir,

In your last letter, you graciously pointed out that I made an unfortunate scientific error by sketching "a far-fetched and superfluous bony trunk" on the elephant's skeleton on page 10 of my last book.

As you are no doubt quite busy juggling your tasks at the museum, you probably read through this work too quickly. Nowhere does it make reference to an elephant, but a cat.

Though you may see things differently, I believe cats, as a general rule, don't have trunks.

I myself had accepted this fact until I discovered that my cat definitely had one.

Only an X ray can categorically determine whether this trunk contains bones or not. Unfortunately, my illustrator's income is too meager to cover this expensive veterinary procedure.

As soon as I receive more detailed information on this subject, I shall, without fail, pass it on to you. Until then, I remain, sincerely yours,

Gilles Bachelet

My cat always forgets to wipe his feet before stepping all over my work.

My cat thinks that he has perfect aim when he goes to the bathroom.

Aside from that, my cat is clean.

Very clean.

Extremely clean.

Almost excessively clean,

bordering on vanity.

Having always lived in a clean and tidy apartment, my cat has never seen a mouse.

Too bad, since he really seems to love other animals.

They say that when cats fall,
they always land on their feet.

Not my cat.

I've painted many portraits of my cat.

But I've never managed to sell one.

Maybe I should have chosen a more colorful cat.

A friend recently gave me a book about cats...

. . .but I wasn't able to determine my cat's breed.